YOU ARE THE PEA, AND I AM THE CARROT

WORDS BY J. THERON ELKINS   PICTURES BY PASCAL LEMAITRE

ABRAMS BOOKS FOR YOUNG READERS
NEW YORK

The art in this book was made with
pencil and colored on a computer.

Library of Congress Cataloging-in-Publication Data

Elkins, J. Theron
You are the pea, and I am the carrot / J. Theron Elkins ; [illustrated by Pascal Lemaitre].
p. cm.
Summary: A friendship between two very compatible people is described in terms of foods
that go together, such as funnel cake with powdered sugar, or salsa and chips.
[1. Stories in rhyme. 2. Friendship—Fiction. 3. Food—Fiction.] I. Lemaitre, Pascal, ill. II. Title.
PZ8.3.E444You 2013
[E]—dc23
2012039868

ISBN: 978-1-4197-0850-3

Text copyright © 2013 J. Theron Elkins
Illustrations copyright © 2013 Pascal Lemaitre
Book design by Chad W. Beckerman

Printed and bound in China
10 9 8 7 6 5 4 3 2 1

Abrams Books for Young Readers are available at special discounts when purchased in quantity for
premiums and promotions as well as fundraising or educational use. Special editions can also be
created to specification. For details, contact specialsales@abramsbooks.com or the address below.

THE ART OF BOOKS SINCE 1949
115 West 18th Street
New York, NY 10011
www.abramsbooks.com

For (and about) my only
sweet pea, Isabelle

—J.T.E.

For Manou, my *kuy teav*,
and Maëlle, my *amok trey*

— P.L.

You are the pea,

And I am the carrot.

I am the butter, and you are the bread.

Warm fried chicken served with mashed potatoes,

Zesty dressing on a cold lettuce bed.

We belong together.
Combined, we make a dish.
We're made for one another,
'Cause together we're delish.

You are the steak, and I am the pepper.

I am the burger, and you are the chips.

Cubes of ice cooling a glass of sweet tea,

Toasty 'mallows on a graham cracker crisp.

We belong together.
A match this good is rare.
Together we're just better.
We're an appetizing pair.

You are the 'jacks, and I am the syrup.

I am the biscuit, and you are the jam.

A cup of yogurt with fresh blueberries,

Sunny-side eggs with Canadian ham.

We belong together.
Mouthwatering are we.
We complement each other.
We're the perfect recipe.

You are the scoop, and I am the sprinkles.

I am the cherry, and you are the cream.

A swirly mix of two awesome flavors,

Like caramel chip and vanilla bean.

We belong together.
We're such a tasty sweet.
We're yummy, scrumptious morsels.
We're the perfect little treat.

You are the dog, and I am the relish.

I am the mac, and you are the cheese.

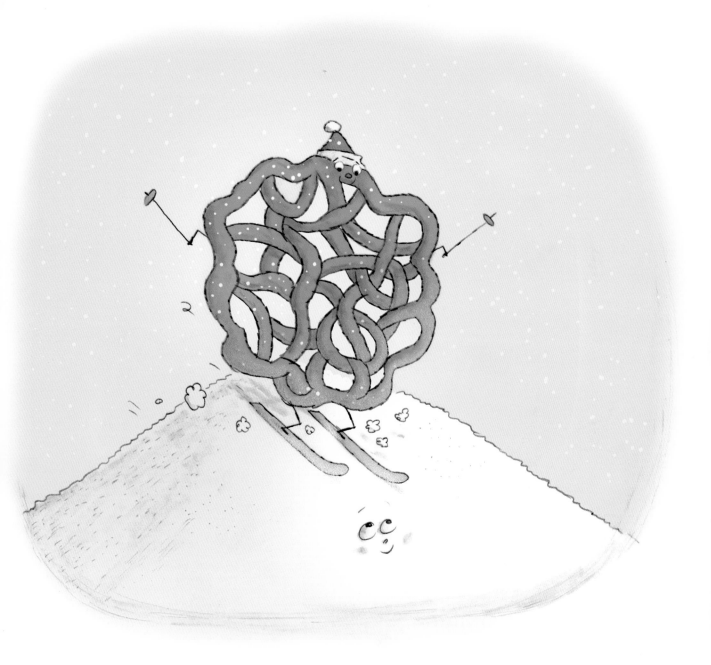

A funnel cake with powdered sugar,

A wooden spoon for a lemonade freeze.

We belong together.
Apart we don't make sense.
Our hearts are mixed together.
Better matches don't exist.

For you are the peanut to my butter,

And I am the salsa to your chip.

'Cause we will always belong together
And will never—ever—*ever*—be split!